# On the Bus

Written by Suzy Senior
Illustrated by Parwinder Singh

**Collins**

This bus will go to the shops.

# Get the bus tickets.

5

Put the things on the rack.

Then sit!

7

The bus zips along.

Ring this bell to get off.

buzz

Quick, hop off.

That was fun.

/w/

06

#  After reading

**Letters and Sounds:** Phase 3

**Word count:** 41

**Focus phonemes:** /w/ /z/ zz /qu/ /sh/ /th/ /ng/ /nk/

**Common exception words:** the, go, to, you, put, was, we

**Curriculum links:** Personal, social and emotional development; Understanding the world

**Early learning goals:** Reading: read and understand simple sentences; use phonic knowledge to decode regular words and read them aloud accurately; read some common irregular words

## Developing fluency

- Your child may enjoy hearing you read the book.
- Read pages 2 and 4 with expression, then take turns to read a page, with your child reading page 5. Check your child uses a different voice for the speech bubble, and reads page 7 with extra emphasis because of the exclamation mark.

## Phonic practice

- Focus on the letter sounds /ng/, /nk/ and /sh/.
- Ask your child to sound out and blend the following:
  th/i/ng/s    c/a/sh    th/a/nk    r/i/ng    r/u/sh
- Say the words and challenge your child to spell them out loud.
- Look at the "I spy sounds" pages (14–15) together. Take turns to find a word in the picture containing a /w/ or /x/ sound. (e.g. *window, wellies, waving, watch*; *T-Rex, fox, six*)

## Extending vocabulary

- On page 8, ask your child what **zips** means. (e.g. *races, hurries, goes fast*) Can they describe a thing that is a different sort of **zip**? (e.g. *a fastening on trousers*)
- On page 12, ask your child what **hop off** means. (e.g. *get off, jump off* ) Can they describe a time when they have hopped? (e.g. *in a hopping race, when skipping*)